MW00889846

To all bakers who share their yummy talent with others,
especially Mary and Sean— the young bakers in my life. —T.S.

To all the dog and cat lovers out there, thank you for adopting
the furbabies to be part of your families! Continue to love and be kind. — P.J.

With many thanks to: Candice Hazlett Jensen, Amy Dyche, Marty, Rachel, Matthew,
and Madeline for their support and encouragement.

KNEADING A WINNING IDEA

WRITTEN BY TERRI SABOL   **ILLUSTRATED BY PEI JEN**

Never give up on your dreams!

Ben sighs. "Why do I even bother? I don't want to lose to Sofía and her Abuela's Mexican sweet bread for the third year in a row. Though I would love for my buttermilk biscuits to finally be featured on our lunch menu."

Ben's cat, Miss Kitty, purrs.

Ben's dad asks, "Are you going to enter the contest again?"

"I don't know. Maybe with a different bread?" Ben replies.

"Why? Everyone loves your biscuits."

"Not as much as they love Sofía's bread," Ben says.

"Is there anything you can do to enrich or improve the recipe a little?" Dad suggests, "I'd be happy to sample it."

Ben experiments with his recipe. He adds a tablespoon of cinnamon. He gives his dad a biscuit to taste. Dad smiles and politely shakes his head.

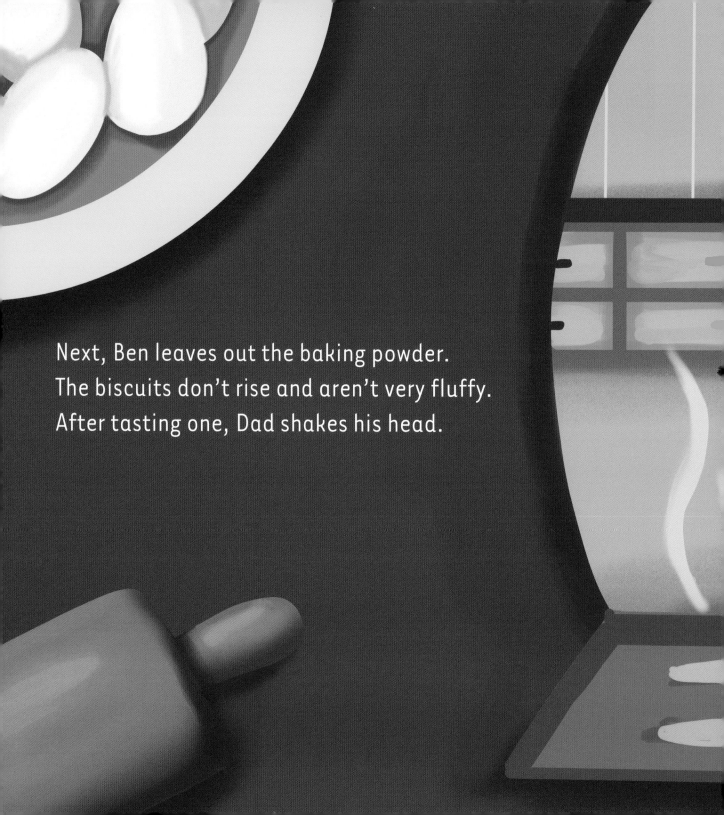

Next, Ben leaves out the baking powder.
The biscuits don't rise and aren't very fluffy.
After tasting one, Dad shakes his head.

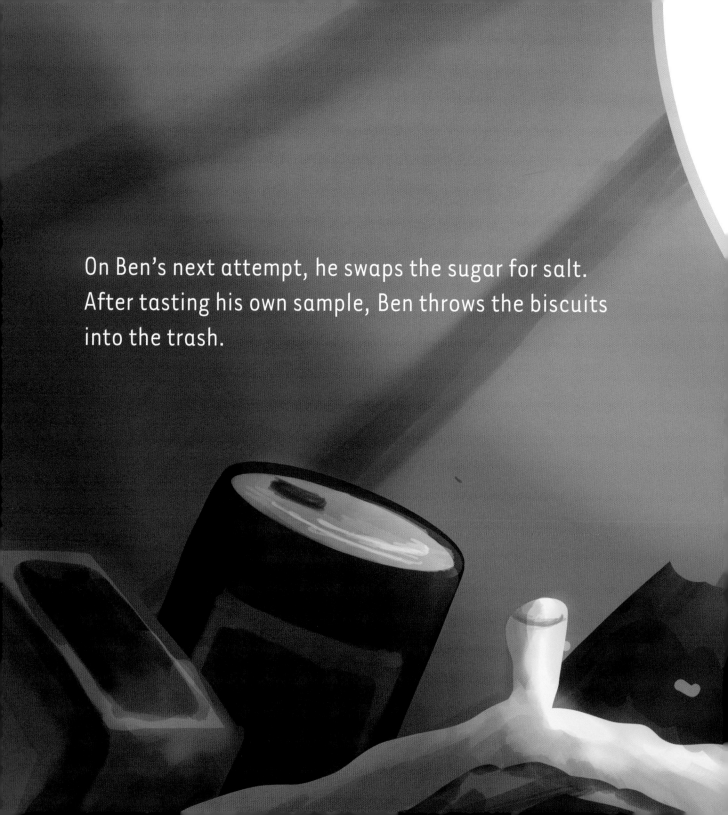

On Ben's next attempt, he swaps the sugar for salt.
After tasting his own sample, Ben throws the biscuits
into the trash.

Ben looks at the flyer again as he pets Miss Kitty. "Today's the last day, and I've tried everything. What's the point of even entering the contest with the same old bread?"

Miss Kitty purrs and kneads his lap. "Don't you ever get tired of kneading my leg?" Miss Kitty keeps on kneading.

"Wait a second! Miss Kitty, where did you learn to knead like that?"

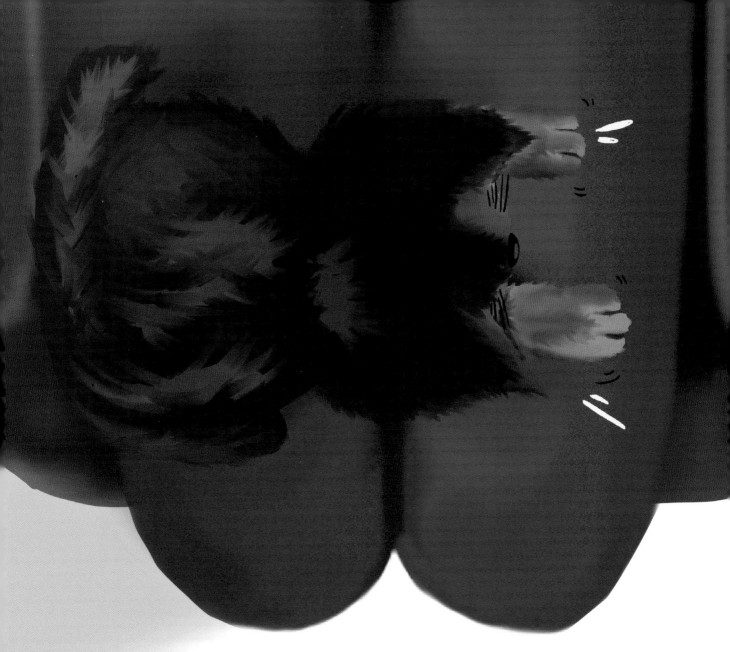

Miss Kitty alternates her two front paws and presses them into his leg. It is a rhythmic back-and-forth motion between her left and right paws.

Ben tries out his new hand-kneading method on the recipe. Usually he uses the electric mixer to knead the dough, but the hand-kneading method that Miss Kitty taught him is definitely more fun. Ben finishes kneading and forms the dough into biscuits. He places them in the oven to bake.

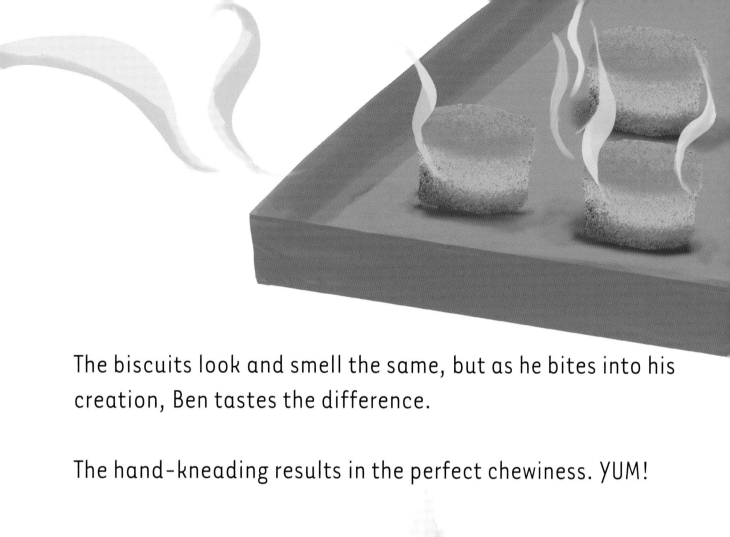

The biscuits look and smell the same, but as he bites into his creation, Ben tastes the difference.

The hand-kneading results in the perfect chewiness. YUM!

Ben gives a biscuit to his dad to try. "Wow, what did you do differently? What's your secret ingredient?"

"If I tell you, then it won't be a secret."

"Well whatever you did, please keep doing it. This is delicious!" Dad exclaims.

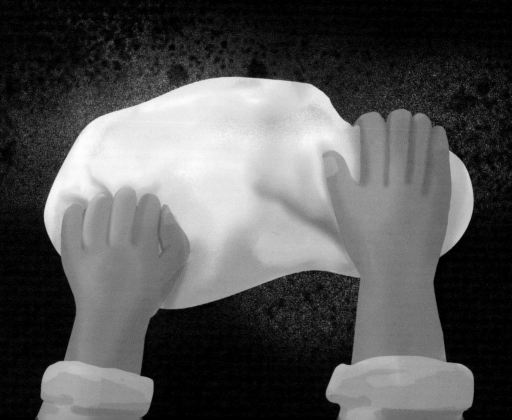

On contest day, as Ben turns in his special hand-kneaded biscuits to the judges, Sofía turns in her Mexican sweet bread.

Sofía laughs, "You made your biscuits again? I thought you might try something new. Good luck."

They enjoy tasting all of the baked bread submissions.

"The runner-up is Sofía and her Mexican sweet bread. The first place winner is... Ben and his delicious buttermilk biscuits!"

Ben can't believe his ears! "Thank you everyone.
I can't wait for the whole school to eat them every week —
You will love them!"

Sofía finishes her biscuit, "Congratulations, Ben. Your biscuits are really good. You deserve 1st place."

At home, Miss Kitty rubs her face on Ben's blue ribbon, and then kneads his lap.

Fluffy Buttermilk Biscuits

Prep Time: 20 Mins
Bake Time: 11 Mins
Yield: Makes about 18 biscuits

Ingredients

- 3 1/2 cups self-rising soft wheat flour
- 2 1/4 teaspoons baking powder
- 2 1/4 teaspoons sugar
- 1/4 cup shortening
- 1/4 cup butter, chilled and cut into pieces
- 1 1/2 cups buttermilk
- 1/2 to 1 cup self-rising flour
- 1 tablespoon butter, melted

How to Make It

Step 1

Combine first 3 ingredients until well blended. Cut in shortening and chilled butter with a pastry blender or a fork until crumbly. Add buttermilk, stirring just until dry ingredients are moistened.

Step 2

Turn dough out onto a well-floured surface; sprinkle with 1/2 cup self-rising flour. Knead 20 to 25 times, adding up to 1/2 cup additional flour until dough is smooth and springy to touch.

Step 3

Pat dough into a 3/4-inch-thick circle (about 8 1/2 inches round). Cut dough with a well-floured 2 1/2 inch round cutter, making 12 biscuits. Place on ungreased baking sheets. Knead remaining dough together 3 or 4 times; repeat procedure, making 6 more biscuits. Lightly brush tops with melted butter.

Step 4

Bake at 500° for 9 to 11 minutes or until golden.

Adapted from the Southern Living June 2007 recipe
Fluffy buttermilk biscuits recipe. (2007, May 22). MyRecipes. Retrieved February 14, 2021, from https://www.myrecipes.com/recipe/fluffy-buttermilk-biscuits

For information regarding permission, write to

Burning the Midnight Oil
Publishing

1860 FM 359 #173, Richmond, TX 77406 USA.

ISBN: 978-1-946428-21-9
Library of Congress Control Number: 2021901794

Book Design by Pei Jen
Cover Design by Pei Jen and Praise Saflor
Edited by Tamara Rittershaus

Printed in the USA
Signature Book Printing, www.sbpbooks.com

Terri Sabol

AUTHOR

Although Terri Sabol would like to say this story was inspired by her own love of baking, it was instead inspired by her cat's constant kneading.

Other books written by Terri Sabol include the *Oscar and Emmy Series* and *Green With Envy*.

Pei Jen

ILLUSTRATOR

Although Pei Jen has no talent in baking, she absolutely adores great bakers and their homemade cookies! She is grateful to be part of the creative team in making this book, and she hopes it will make readers smile.

Other books illustrated by Pei Jen include *Green With Envy, The Lonely Cloud Series,* and *When the Clock Strikes Series.*